Henry Clark Barlow

Francesca da Rimini

Henry Clark Barlow

Francesca da Rimini

Reprint of the original, first published in 1859.

1st Edition 2022 | ISBN: 978-3-37513-256-9

Verlag (Publisher): Salzwasser Verlag GmbH, Zeilweg 44, 60439 Frankfurt, Deutschland
Vertretungsberechtigt (Authorized to represent): E. Roepke, Zeilweg 44, 60439 Frankfurt, Deutschland
Druck (Print): Books on Demand GmbH, In de Tarpen 42, 22848 Norderstedt, Deutschland

FRANCESCA DA RIMINI,

HER LAMENT, AND VINDICATION;

WITH

A BRIEF NOTICE OF THE MALATESTI,

E'l Mastin vecchio, e'l nuovo da Verrucchio.

BY

HENRY CLARK BARLOW, M.D.

ACCADEMICO CORRESPONDENTE DE' QUIRITTI DI ROMA,

ETC. ETC.

LONDON:

DAVID NUTT, 270, STRAND.

MDCCCLIX.

FRANCESCA DA RIMINI.

"Amor, ch'al cor gentil ratto s'apprende,
Prese costui della bella persona,
Che mi fu tolta, e il MONDO ancor m'offende."

INFERNO, CANTO V. v. 100-102.

In that memorable year of revolutions, when
Italy, electrified with new life, resolved to assert
her independence and to vindicate her ancient
renown, when the Sovereign Pontiff, seemingly
disposed to lead the way, and to inaugurate a new
era of Italian unity, heard himself saluted as the
VELTRO of Dante, there was, in the venerable city
of the Exarchs, an enterprising Letterato preparing
a new edition of the Divina Commedia, with the
prepossessing title—"*Edizione Ravegnana, fatta per
uso degl' Italiani rigenerati da Pio Nono.*"

This gentleman was the Abbate Mauro Ferranti, who, moved by the patriotic motive that the resting place of Dante's remains might send forth to the world a text of his immortal poem more perfect than any which had preceded it, resolved to introduce into this edition, prepared expressly for the use of his regenerated countrymen, certain new readings from the two Codici of the Divina Commedia preserved in the Biblioteca Classense.

One of these Codici, in that surpassing episode of the loves and deaths of Francesca da Rimini and Paolo Malatesta da Verruchio, instead of the ordinary reading of the 102nd verse—

"Che mi fu tolta, e il modo ancor m'offende;"

has

"Che mi fu tolta, e il *mondo* ancor m'offende;"

and the other Codice, which is somewhat the elder of the two, and of the second half of the fourteenth century, has the same reading as a variante, in the margin.

This supposed discovery, for such it was deemed, was hailed with applause; and from the correspondence which took place on the subject, between the Signor Abbate and certain distinguished letterati, it appeared that the reading *mondo* was as new to them as it was to him.

Gio. Battista Niccolini remarked that although he approved of it, yet he doubted if the reading of the volgata could be changed on the authority of two codici only. To Giovanni Marchetti it was also quite new, and he stated in reply to the letter of the Abbate, that the more he considered it the better he liked it. Carlo Troya also greatly approved of it, and said—" Confesso che l'antica lezione del ' *modo* ancor m'offende,' m'era paruta sempre, Dio mel perdoni, una riempitura di verso, tutto che a difenderla, m'andassi dicendo che Francesca si dolesse d'essere stata uccisa in istato di peccato, e senza confessione." " Piace," he added, " ad altri ancoro, che ho interrogato, e che si sentono molto avanti nello studio di Dante."

In a villeggiatura from Florence, that year, I visited Ravenna, the Mecca of all Dantofili, to pay my homage at the Prophet's tomb, and on this occasion had the satisfaction of making the acquaintance of the learned Abbate, of seeing his book in the press, and looking at the Codici in the public library from which the new reading had been taken. Since then, however, I have found that the reading,

" Che mi fu tolta, e il *mondo* ancor m'offende ; "

is by no means rare, but, on the contrary, is very frequently met with.

Of forty-two Codici examined by me in the library of the Vatican, and other Roman libraries, *fourteen* were found with *mondo*, that is, half the number of those which had *modo*.

Among the former, in the Vatican library, were the Codici Nos. 365, 367, 2864, 4776, 7566 and 2863. In the Corsini library, the Codici Nos. 56, 60 and 1354. In the Barberini library, the Codici Nos. 2190, and 1526. In the Chegiana, the Codice No. 109. In the Angelica, the Codice No. 10⅞; and in the Minerva, the Codice d. IV. d. In this last, and in the Vatican Codice 2863, the reading was

" Che mi fu tolta *al mondo* che m'offende."

In the Corsini Codice, No. 1354, the verse was written,

" Che mi fu tolta *al mondo* c'or m'offende."

Mondo instead of *modo* occurs in other Codici which I have seen, as in that in the public library at Dresden, in which, however, the *n* has been crossed out; also in certain Codici at Paris, and in London. The Codice Gradonico, in the Gambalunghiana, at Rimini, has also the reading, " e il *mondo* ancor m'offende."

As regards Codici, therefore, there is abundant authority for the reading *mondo*; and probably, in many instances, where we find *modo*, this latter is to be attributed to the haste or negligence of transcribers, who have omitted to put the hyphen over the *o* to indicate the absence of the *n*, this little mark being generally the sole orthographical difference between the two words. A remarkable instance of this omission occurs in the famous Codice di Santa Croce, at Florence, Inferno, Canto III, v. 49, where we have *modo* for *mondo*—" *Fama di loro il modo*

esser non lasser." In the 75 v. of the IV Canto of the
Inferno, we almost invariably find *modo* for *mondo*,
which latter the context shows to be the required
reading, as the poet is referring to a particular
locality where the poets and philosophers of anti-
quity are placed apart from the "mal mondo" of
the common herd, who occupy the "selva di spiriti
spessi."—and as we find in the Codice Urbinato,
No. 365, in the Vatican library—

"Che dal mondo degli altri gli diparte."

That the omission of the hyphen was the origin
of the reading *modo* in the episode of Francesca da
Rimini derives support also from the fact, that
although none of the early printed editions have
the reading *mondo* in the text, yet the earliest two
with commentaries, the VENDELINIANA and the
NIDOBEATINA, have *mondo* in the explanation of the
text, and this explanation is very like that in the
commentary of the Codice Gradonico with which
the text agrees. The commentator here explains—
"Onde quello suo conpagno abiando come è decto
il core gentile si se inamoro di lei et de la persona
di lei. La quale persona suso al mondo gli fu tolta,
zioè che a male morte de gladio morio, apresso dice
chel mondo ancora la offende. Altro qui non vole dire
se no de la nominanza et fama, et che di tale cosa
ancora el mondo mal ne ragiona."

The corresponding passages in the Vendeliniana
and in the Nidobeatina, are as follows:

" Siche quel suo cōpagno avēdo il cuore gētile sinamoro della persona di lei, la quale persona li fu tolta al mōdo, cioè che morì di gladio. Et dice che ancora il mondo gli offende cioè la nominanza et fama."

" Ora dice la conditione del suo cōpagno, cavea lo core gentile e che in li cori gentili saprende facilmente amore, e pero se iāmorò di lei, che li fu tolta, zoè che fu morta di gladio, e ancora li offende al mondo per la fama e nominanza." · ·

The commentary in the Vendeliniana, once attributed to Benvenuto da Imola, and now ascribed to Jacopo della Lana, Bolognese, as it is, next to that by Jacopo di Dante, the oldest extant, and of far more importance, is of the highest authority for the reading *mondo*.

In the British Museum Codice, No. 10,317, although the text has *modo*, the postilla is upon *mondo*, and the explanation is "fama hujus facti."

In the Vatican Codice, No. 367, we have a fuller explanation of this—"fama mea offendit me, quia dicor mortua fuisse per adulterium, et causa mei mortuum fuisse Paulum," and with this the text, as it should do, corresponds,

" Che mi fu tolta, e il MONDO ancor m'offende."

In the latter part of the thirteenth century, a domestic tragedy was enacted in the palace of a nobleman of Rimini, which, though it produced a very painful impression at the time, yet does not appear to have been recorded by any contemporary chronicler. It was a tragedy perpetrated by an enraged and jealous husband in the chamber of his wife.

On the following morning two bodies were carried forth for interment,—they were those of his wife and of his brother. This is all that was known for certain: they were said to have been slain together, and it was reported in the act of adultery.

There was no judicial investigation, no collecting of evidence: whether the deed was unpremeditated homicide, or revengeful murder, were questions which none ventured to ask—none dared to inquire. The victims were deeply commiserated, and there was an universal mourning at their miserable deaths, but there was no investigation of the terrible deed: he who had committed it was powerful, and had his friends, who would endeavour to shield him from reprobation, and lessen the infamy of the act.

Reports were spread, which in time came to be written down, and subsequently were raised to the rank of registered facts, and so passed current in the world as matters of genuine history, but with no better foundation of truth than the representations of those who were disposed to favor the guilty, and of others who had no opportunity of knowing what the true circumstances were.

Yet, though this tragical event found no formal recorder of the time to transmit to posterity the character of his own conviction, the fact, like a seed sown on a fertile soil, fell on the love-inspired soul of a young and noble Florentine, and there, subject to those latent operations known only to the soul and to its Author, germinating in the virgin force of a genuine life-giving poetry, in due season put forth its strength, and raised to the perpetuity of universal fame the name of Francesca da Rimini.

Then did this domestic tragedy become of historical interest, then were inquiries made, and particulars sought after, and with the ever-extending circle of the wide-spreading renown of the Divina Commedia and its immortal author, that, which but for Dante, would soon have subsided in the silence of the grave, and have been for ever forgotten, acquired an importance to which no similarly sad incident had ever attained.

And what were these particulars ? Mere reports are unworthy of reproduction, and Dante did not write to gratify a vulgar curiosity. With a profound knowledge of human nature, and with the art of a consummate master—as in that other pathetic story of revenge and suffering, the episode of the Conte Ugolino, and the innocent victims of an archbishop's unmeasured malice—Dante reveals, as from the lips of the chief sufferer, what otherwise, reader, thou couldst not have heard—

"Però quel che non puoi avere inteso."

The account of the first root of Francesca's fatal love may be pure poetic invention, meant to point a moral, no less than to adorn a tale; but, though we reject the narrative, we must not refuse to receive the impression it was intended to convey, nor the evidence therein set forth of Francesca's character.

From what Dante relates, we may gather that the love of Francesca for Paolo was not a sensual passion, but a generous sentiment and commendable, a something peculiar "*al cor gentil,*" and such as Dante himself had cherished for the object of his own tender attachment, when he so innocently sang,

"Amore e cor gentil sono una cosa."

Francesca, however, did not appear in visions to Paolo, but came in her own real, beautiful, bodily presence; yet she had no suspicion of anything dangerous, much less of anything wrong; and, for their mutual amusement, read with Paolo a romance of the character of which she was entirely ignorant. Poor Francesca! the fatal passage came, and the consciousness of their attachment was betrayed by a kiss,—it was well for Dante that nothing of this sort ever happened between himself and Beatrice, at least so far as we know. What followed, we are not told, only that they read no more that day together, and Francesca brands the book and the author of it with an odious name, such as she felt they fully deserved,

" Galeotto fu' il libro e chi lo scrisse."

There is a virtuous indignation in these words, which, as the poet relates, much affected the shade of Paolo, for, penetrated with compunction at the recital, he wept bitterly.

Boccaccio, who desired to walk as much as possible in the footsteps of his master, has left us an account of the story of Francesca, such as he had received it, probably, from Ser Piero di Messer Giardino of Ravenna, who had been an intimate friend of Dante, and had furnished Giovanni with other particulars; and this account is at least as deserving of credit as the story of the loves of Dante and Beatrice, which Boccaccio has related so much to the satisfaction of biographers and commentators, that they almost invariably follow it as a matter of unquestionable fact.

Boccaccio, in his Commentary, states more circumstantially than any other writer, the particulars of Francesca's unfortunate love, beginning from the day when she first saw Paolo in her father's palace at Rimini, and was given to understand that he had come to woo and to wed her for himself alone, and "incontanente in lui pose l'animo e l'amor suo." After the marriage ceremony she was conducted to Rimini, and it was only on the following morning that she discovered the deception which had been practised upon her, in the substitution of Paolo's deformed brother, Gianciotto, in the place of him to whom she had given her heart.

There is another version of this portion of the story, in which it is said, that Gianciotto came to Ravenna as the representative of Paulo, then a widower, to whom Francesca had been promised by her mother, but, seeing her great beauty, he resolved to have her for himself, and, as her relations did not venture to oppose his will, Francesca became his wife, to the great vexation of herself and of her mother. Such is the notice found in the "Chiose sopra Dante," by Lami erroneously attributed to Boccaccio, and printed at Florence in 1846. Landino also alludes to this report, and Rossi, in his history of Ravenna, relates it at considerable length. Clementini, on the contrary, states that in 1275, Guido da Polenta being hard pressed by the Ghibellins, applied to Malatesta for assistance, who sent him his son Giovanni with one hundred horse, and that it was as a reward for this service that Guido gave him his daughter in marriage.

It matters little what was the political motive that induced Guido da Polenta to give the beautiful Francesca to the deformed but energetic son of Malatesta, whether to create an alliance or to strengthen one, though most probably the latter, for both families were of the Guelf faction, and this was not the only connection between them, as Ber-

Dante and the family of Francesca, anterior to the period when, at the court of her nephew, Guido Novello, in Ravenna, the poet ended his weary pilgrimage, honored, esteemed, and loved.

Signor Mercuri, a Roman Letterato, has recently endeavoured to show, that Dante was the guest of Francesca's father at Ravenna, as early, probably, as 1302; and, that during the remainder of his life, this city was his recognized home, rather than any other, (see the Giornale Arcadico, Tom. cxli.) The evidence, however, is not conclusive, nor is the statement very probable; but, although the Polentani were Guelfs, and Dante became a declared Ghibellin, when all hopes of a political change had ceased, all prospects of a return to Florence perished, and all other friends had failed him, the family of Francesca received the poet gladly, and felt gratified by his presence.

Can we then believe that Dante, having the choice of words before him—words equally well suited to his verse, and so alike in written characters that they might easily be mistaken the one for the other—and having the love and regard for the family at heart, no less than a personal sentiment of respect and pity for the memory of Francesca, would select that word which might be taken as a confirmation of the world's worst reports, rather than that other word, which, if it did not clear Francesca of the guilt imputed to her, would at least render the charge doubtful, and cover the accusation with an impenetrable veil?

In Francesca, Dante has depicted the force of woman's love stronger than death. Francesca appears before us as one who, by her gentleness, her resignation, and her piety, is more fitted for the blessedness of heaven than the bufera of hell. In the short account which she gives of her tragical death, there is a candour, a modesty, a delicacy of sentiment, a shrinking from conscious impropriety, united with an amount of womanly feeling—let cynics call it weakness if they will, this weakness is woman's strength—which excite our deepest sympathy, and convince our reason that Francesca was more sinned against than sinning.

But to complete this interesting portrait, another trait of womanly feeling required to be added, a trait inseparable from the character of Francesca as here depicted, namely, a regard for her reputation in the world.

Dante was too consummate a master of human nature to forget this, he was too generous to omit it. The evil report abroad in the world touching the occasion and manner of Francesca's death must afflict, must offend her, she remembers the past, she also sees into the future:—

" Cotanto ancor ne splende il sommo Duce ; "

and thus beholding, speaks in the present time, which is adapted to both, and complains, as well she might—" *il mondo ancor m' offende.*"

By the ordinary reading, in which Francesca,

B

alluding to the separation of her beautiful person from her living soul, is made to say

" Che mi fu tolta, e il *modo* ancor m'offende,"

not only is this essential trait of her womanly character omitted, but we have in its place an expression which may be construed as confirming the most offensive reports in circulation, itself also an offence, and showing how justly Francesca had reason to complain, " *il mondo ancor m' offende.*"

With the reading *modo* the sense is not complete, something requires to be understood, and may be misunderstood; Boccaccio gave it one meaning, Buti another, and Ugo Foscolo would give it a sense different from both. This reading is in fact a bad reading, it is even worse than a third reading found in the Codice, No. 7251², of the National Library at Paris,

" Che mi fu tolta, e il *moto* ancor m'offende,"

in which, if *moto* might be taken for *motivo*, the meaning would be much improved.

But let *mondo* be put in the place of *modo*, or let the reading be

" Che mi fu tolta *al mondo* ch' or m' offende ;"

and we have not only the recognition of the fact that the world did speak evil of Francesca, but we have also this other fact noticed that in so doing the world did her wrong, and that she felt it.

Dante thus admits the fact of the report that Francesca and Paolo were slain together in the act of adultery, but not the truth of it; and Dante is no common chronicler; he is the only known contemporary writer who mentions the circumstance of their deaths, and he it was who gave to the subject such alto relievo, that sculptured on the living rock it lasts,

" E durera quanto il mondo lontana."

Dante was the intimate associate of Francesca's nearest and dearest relatives, he would, therefore, know the truth as known by them, or at least as believed by them, and his version of it would correspond; of this there cannot be a doubt, any more than there can be a doubt that to the last the Polentani were his best and firmest friends.

The story of Francesca da Rimini and of Paolo Malatesta, as narrated by chroniclers and early historians, is singularly deficient in consistency, and is wanting in the precision and exactitude of those fundamental particulars of dates and places on which alone unquestionable reliance can be laid.

Francesca's marriage is placed in 1275, her death, in the first edition of Rossi's History of Ravenna, in 1276 (so Tonnini). Ubaldo Branca, who wrote in 1474, in his unedited chronicle, places the latter between 1288 and September 1289, and is followed by Clementini. The chronicle of Pesaro places it in 1296. Marco Battaglia, the earliest Riminese chronicler, who wrote in, or after 1352 (see Raccolta Calogeriana, Tom. XLIV.), mentions it incidentally after the death of Malatesta, which took place in 1312. The Anonimo Riminese, who wrote after 1385 (see his Chronicle apud Muratori "Rerum Italicarum Scriptores," Tom. XV.), also places it under the year 1312, when Malatestino had taken his father's place in the Government of Rimini. "Fu fatto il detto Malatestino Signore d'Arimino, et era tanto amato che non si porria contare. Accadde caso così fatto, che 'l detto Zanne Sciancado suo fratello trovò Paolo suo fratello con la donna sua, et ebbelo morto subito lui, e la donna sua." This author, who enters more fully into the history, of the Malatesta family than does Marco Battaglia, and is a more credible writer, says not a word about Francesca having been taken in adultery.

It is remarkable that not one of the early chroniclers, except Tomasso Diplovatazio, in the chronicle of Pesaro, intimates where the deaths of Francesca and Paolo were believed to have happened. He says, after mentioning the circumstance under 1296, " Et hoc fuit Pisauri in Palatio Communis juxta

Portam Gattuli, quæ postea fuit Dominorum de Malatestis, et nostris temporibus ivi venditur sal. Aliqui dicunt fuisse Anno Domini 1312, postquam dominus Malatestinus fuit factus Dominus Arimini. Aliqui tamen dicunt fuisse Arimini in domo magna quæ (est) in capite plateæ magnæ, qui nunc possidetur ab Angelo cive Arimini."

Benvenuto da Imola, who wrote in 1375, is quoted as the earliest authority for placing the event in September, 1289, but in the abridgement of his commentary, printed by Muratori (Dissertationes, Tom. I.), this is not found, which throws a doubt upon its exactitude. Nor can Ubaldo Branca here be trusted, for he states that Gianciotto departed this life in 1317, thirteen years after he had been dead. Carlo Troya, however, is very confident on the subject; in a letter to Monsignore Marino Marini (Giornale Arcadico, Tom. CXXIX.), he says, "Io la pongo, senza niun dubbio, nel giorno 4 di Settembre, 1289." This is very precise, but he does not name the hour. Carlo Troya was once equally certain that the event took place in Pesaro, until convinced by the eloquence of Monsignore, that it happened in Santarcangelo. It was perpetrated in Rimini, as stated by Boccaccio, and confirmed by Benvenuto da Imola, but not in 1312, for Gianciotto had then been dead eight years; nor in 1289, for it would appear that he had married his second wife, Ginevrasina, in 1288 (see Tonini "Memorie Storiche intorno a Francesca da Rimini,"

1852); but rather in or soon after 1276, the last year in which we have any well-authenticated notice of Paolo. Boccaccio states that the tragical event occurred at Rimini, during the absence of Gianciotto to a neighbouring city as Podestà, but Gianciotto did not go as Podestà to Pesaro until 1290 or 1291; in 1276, however, he went as Podestà to Forlì. From 1288 to September 1289, Gianciotto, and also his father, and probably others of his family, were exiles from Rimini, and in open rebellion against the authority of the Comune, circumstances which render it almost impossible that the event could have taken place in the Palace of the Malatesti in that city.

Seven miles from Rimini, on the via Emilia, at the foot of a range of hills that rise with grateful verdure from the plain, stood for many centuries a Christian church dedicated to the Militant Archangel St. Michael; a population of country people collected about it, who, requiring more protection than their patron could afford them, notwithstanding his influential position " of Celestial Armies Chief," raised fortifications for their better defence, and enclosed their little village with a wall; in time this village grew into a town, and having had the honour, in 1705, of giving birth to Pope Ganganelli (Clement XIV.), was raised in 1828 to the rank of a city, La Città di S. Archangelo. In 1288, when the Malatesti were exiled from Rimini, this place was a strong castello of the Riminesi, which the bold Gian-

ciotto seized in the name of the Church, and held it as
a place of security for himself and his family, until
September, 1289, when he gave it up to the Eccle-
siastical Legate.

A castle full of soldiers, in the midst of the
hubbub of war, would appear to be little adapted to
the quiet enjoyment of lovers, but Monsignor Marino
Marini thought differently, and certainly, if the
Malatesta tragedy occurred at this time, it is difficult
to conceive how it could have taken place in Rimini,
where it certainly did.   On the 20th of March, 1290,
a sentence of concord was pronounced between the
Comune of Rimini and the various fuorusciti, but
Malatesta and his sons were not at this time re-
admitted to their residence within the city.   In the
pacification no mention is made of Paolo, nor does
his name occur in that threatening edict, by which,
in 1288, Stefano Colonna, the Rector in Romagna,
summoned the members of the Malatesta family,
Malatesta the father, and Gianciotto, and Malatestino,
his sons, to appear before him in Imola, along with
Bernardino and Ostagio, of Polenta, to answer for
having laid siege to Cervia and done much injury
to its citizens.   Paolo was either then dead, or had
no hand in these aggressive doings.

The differences thus found to exist among authors in
the statements of matters which were not secret things,
but facts well known at the time when they occurred,
and which might easily have been verified afterwards,
show that as these chroniclers gave themselves no

trouble to ascertain correctly what they could have known, had they taken the necessary pains, in relating what they could not with equal certainty have known, their testimony is unworthy of credit.

There is another circumstance in which chroniclers and historians are all at variance, though it is a simple question of fact, once perfectly well known: and that is, as regards the wives and children of Malatesta. Malatesta was born in 1212, and lived for upwards of a hundred years; during that time he had more wives than one, and a numerous family. Marco Battaglia says, that by his first wife, Concordia, daughter of the late Imperial Vicar Dominus Arighinus, "ex latere materno de Partitatibus nata," he had three sons, Malatestino, Giovanni, and Paolo; and that by his second wife, Margherita, daughter of Pandolfino of Vicenza, he had Pandolfo. The Anonimo Riminese states, that Malatesta had three wives, the first of whom bore to him Malatestino; the second, Giovanni and Paolo; the third, who was the daughter of Messer Righetto dei Pandolfini da Vicenza, Pandolfo. But Benvenuto da Imola, who wrote ten years earlier, 1375, mentions Malatestino as the third son. Dr. Tonini has demonstrated from authentic documents, that Giovanni, Paolo, and Malatestino were the sons of Concordia, and born in this order; and that Pandolfo was born of Margherita, daughter of Pandolfo di Pesce dei Paltonieri da Montesilice, the last wife of Malatesta, and married to him in 1266.

Fra Giovanni da Serravalle, Prince and Bishop of Fermo, writing in 1415, for the information of the Prelates assembled at the Council of Constance, states that Pandolfus was Malatesta's *eldest* son. "Brutto fallo" of Serravalle, exclaims Dr. Tonini, but not his only one.

The Cav. Cesare Clementini, in his "Raccolto istorico della fondatione di Rimini, e dell' origine e vite de' Malatesti," 1677, a book dedicated with exemplary piety to the Queen of Heaven and the saintly protectors of Rimini, adheres to the statement in the chronicle of Marco Battaglia, that Malatesta had only two wives, Concordia and afterwards Margherita. He says, that notwithstanding - the assertions of the chronicles of Urbino, of Pesaro, of Ubaldo Branca, and others, and the commonly-received opinion that Malatesta had three wives—"io dallo stromento dotale di Margherita, dall' altro di mancipazione, fatto da Malatesta à Figliuoli, et à Nipoti, e dal suo proprio testamento ricappo, che con due si congiunse, che furono Concordia, e poi Margherita, figliuola di Pandolfo de' Paltroneri da Monselice." We are told as clearly as possible by Marco Battaglia, that Concordia was the daughter of the Imperial Vicar: "Interim Dominus Arighinus Imperii Vicarius in Romandiola Arimini moritur: et quasi ibi faciebat continue moram suam; de quo remansit unica Filia nomine Concordia, ex latere materno de Partitatibus nata, quam dictus Dominus Malatesta habuit in uxorem, cum maxima pecunia, et possessionibus infinitis, Giovediam, Sanctum Maurum, et alia loca plurima infinita, et hic incepit esse Magnus, et dives, et in Arimino quasi de majoribus nominabatur." This is related as anterior to 1248, when the affairs of the empire began to decline, and Malatesta gave his adhesion to the party of the Pope.

The Anonimo Riminese states, that Margherita, the third wife of Malatesta, was the daughter of the late Imperial Vicar, and grand-daughter of Messer Percitade, who had given her to Malatesta to wife, in order to attach him more firmly to the party of the Emperor. Thus it would seem as if these chroniclers had combined to lead posterity astray rather than to enlighten it.

Where there is no contemporary and well accredited record of events, all that we can do towards their verification is to seek the truth by rejecting what is contradictory, and by adhering to those facts only which can be well established by documentary dates—our only sure guides through labyrinths of error and ancient credulity. Proceeding on this principle, we find that the accounts of early authors are not trustworthy in those matters which they might and should have known correctly; and in other matters which they could only have heard as mere reports at second or third hand, their statements are nothing more than the idle talk of one generation transformed into history in a succeeding one. To this class of rumours belongs the popular notion touching the case of Francesca da Rimini, respecting whom, the best informed writers have spoken very cautiously, while the more credulous and garrulous have indulged in their weakness to a culpable extent.

Malatesta was born about 1212. In November 1263, Giovanni and Paolo, his sons, were provided with pensions, at the charge of certain Monasteries in Romagna, "pro sincera devotione quam gerunt ad Romanam Ecclesiam," as it is expressed in the deed; so it is obvious that they were then men grown, and persons whom it was worth conciliating. Their father had many years previously turned from the falling fortunes of the Empire to promote the rising influence of the Church, and these pensions were no doubt intended to confirm his sons in the same policy. We may suppose, therefore, that the eldest son, Giovanni, might then have been at least about two-and-twenty, and Paolo a year or so younger. Their mother, Concordia, was still living, but died before 1266, when Malatesta married Margherita. In 1249, Malatestino was born. Paolo was married to Orabile Beatrice, daughter and heiress of Uberto, Count of Ghiaggiuolo,* in 1269, by whom he had two children, Uberto and Margherita, who received the titles of Count and Countess

---

* Clementini says: "Orabile, chiamata Margherita, figliuola di Uberto de' Malatesti, e sorella d'un altro Uberto, Conte di Ghiaggiuolo.

of Ghiaggiuolo. His elder brother married Francesca, in 1275, as commonly received, and died in 1304; Malatesta died in 1312; Malatestino died in 1317; and Uberto, Paolo's son, was slain in 1324. Now, supposing that Malatesta had been nearly thirty years of age when he married Concordia, Giovanni might have been born in 1241-2; Paolo, in 1242-3; (Malatestino was born six years later) so that in 1269, Paolo would have been about twenty-six; in 1275, about thirty-two; but in 1289, after twenty years of matrimony, he would have been forty-six or forty-seven. Malatesta had numerous children. Giovanni, who was thrice married, had also numerous children; but Paolo, whom his father, from prudent motives, caused to marry early, had only two—only two children in twenty years. This, considering the stock from whence he sprang, would lead us to suspect either that he was a widower at the time of his brother's marriage, as by some conjectured, or that he himself died not long after.

Having seen the little faith that can be placed in the accuracy of chroniclers and ordinary historians, respecting places, persons, and dates: we have now to consider what confidence can be given to them in their assertions touching Francesca herself.

Marco Battaglia, 1352, the earliest of Riminese chroniclers, says " Dominus autem Malatesta vixit annos centum et plus, cui successerunt Malatestinus, et Pandolphus. Paulus autem fuit mortuus per fratrem suum Joannem Zoctum ex causa luxuriæ commissæ cum Francisca Guidonis Julii de Polenta uxore Lanciotti fratris germani Pauli, cum quo Paulus passus est mortem."

Marco Battaglia here seems very ill-informed on the subject about which he is writing, for Joannes Zoctus and Lanciotto (Gianciotto) were not two persons, but one and the same. There is an improved version of this in the 14th chapter of the anonymous Latin Chronicle of the history of Italy from the time of Frederick II. to the year 1354, apud Muratori, R.I.S., Tom. XVI.: "Dominus autem Malatesta vixit annos centum et plus, cui successerunt Malatestinus, et Pandulfus. Paulus autem fuit mortuus per fratrem suum Johannem Gottum causâ luxuriæ." No mention is here made of Francesca: possibly the author had not read the Divina Commedia, or did not think it proper to perpetuate scandal in a purely historical work; or it may be, that he had not sufficient faith in the vulgar story to say more about it. This is clearly the case with the Riminese chronicler who comes next in order—the Anonimo, apud Muratori, R. I. S., Tom. XV., "Cronica Riminese dall' anno 1188 sino all' anno 1385." Whoever the writer may have been, he had read Dante, and speaks of him with much respect, as "il savio Dante." This Anonimo was also more especially the historian of the house of Malatesta, and relates much that is extremely interesting concerning it; but in speaking of the sad tragedy which struck with consternation, horror, and dismay, the two most potent families of the Guelfic party in Romagna—the Polentani and the Malatesti—he observes a caution worthy of all commendation. He states, as before noticed, the fact, and nothing but the fact, as it was and only could be known : " Accadde caso così fatto, che 'l detto Zanne Sciancato suo fratello trovò Paolo suo fratello con la donna sua, et ebbelo morto subito lui, e la donna sua."

Giovanni Boccaccio, who wrote in 1373, and did not care to repeat the idle stories of his predecessors, but relied upon sources of information sought out by himself, expressly states, that he had never heard it said that Francesca had illicit intercourse with Paolo. After relating the deception practised on her, in causing her to believe that Paolo was her real husband, and then taking him from her, he says, " Col quale ella poi si giugnesse, mai non udii dire, se non quello che l' autore ne scrive." Benvenuto da Imola, 1375, apud Muratori, after narrating the reading of the loves of Genevra and Lancilotto, and the kiss which the Queen gave him, adds, " Quum ergo predicti Paulus et Francisca pervenissent ad dictum passum, ita vis istius tractatus vicit ambos, quod continuo deposito libro pervenerunt ad osculum, et ad cetera, quæ sequuntur. Hæc autem in brevi significata Johanni per unum familiarem fuere. Ambos simul in dicta camera, ubi convenerant, mactavit." So that little time elapsed, in the opinion of Benvenuto, between

the fatal kiss and its tragical consequences. The
Prince Bishop of Fermo, writing in 1415, here
indulges his readers with a figure taken from the
Hebrew Bible : " Hoc lecto, Paulus Francescam
intuitus fuit, et in tali intuito palluerunt ambo, et
rubuerunt: tandem habuerunt rem simul. Unus
ex familia Janscianchati hoc videt, et revelavit
domino suo, qui posuit se in istudiis, et breviter
ambos unum super aliam amplexatos interfecit."
We are here reminded of the bold-faced bearing of
Phinehas in his zeal for the Lord; but there is
nothing of this to be found in the relation by
Boccaccio, who states, that Francesca was acci-
dentally killed in her generous attempt to save the
life of Paolo. Ubaldo Branca, 1474, though he
intimates something very similar to the finishing
touches of the Bishop, is careful to qualify it with—
as some people say—" et come se passasse volse dire
per alcuni che lei et Paolo, etc."; thus giving to
this scandal its true character. The Cav. Cesare
Clementini, however, surpasses the Bishop of Fermo
in the liberty he takes with this delicate subject,
and kills the unfortunate lovers in bed, fast asleep
in each other's arms. Having at considerable length
dilated on the circumstances that accompanied and
immediately followed the kiss, which he says did
not displease Francesca, though it evidently took
her by surprise, and having with evident satisfaction
related the amorous glances, the longing desires, and
all the other phenomena of a revealed reciprocal

passion, he adds,—"mà la lunghezza poi del tempo, l'invidia fortuna, ò per dir meglio l'abominevole peccato, del troppo continovato gioco, discopersero l'ascosto, et impudico fuoco al marito, il quale dopò haverlo più volte accennato à Francesca, e chiaritosi del fatto, un giorno trovatoli in letto abbracciati et addormentati, con un sol colpo di spada amendue uccise."

It is to be hoped that the Virgin Queen of Heaven, and the saintly protectors of Rimini, to whom this was dedicated, received the compliment with due allowance for the author's idiosyncracy, or they could not have formed a very favorable opinion of his veracity, nor of his respect for themselves.

But, why thus draw upon the imagination? Why make Francesca appear so different to the person described and pictured by Dante? Why set before us the long libidinous career of a shameless lust, in place of that tender and generous sentiment, che al cor gentil ratto s'apprende? Why thus distort a simple fact? Why seek to destroy the impression which Dante desired to produce? Why thus spoil and pollute his beautiful creation, and reduce it to the level of a disgusting vulgarity? Is the human heart so fallen? Can love not live inseparable from vice? Was not Beatrice once a married woman? The Cav. Clementini, as if sensible of the impropriety of what he had said, immediately adds, "La verità è, che Paolo e Francesca furono uccisi per mano di Giovanni, marito a lei, et a lui fratello, de' quali e dell' amor loro cantò Dante nel quinto del suo inferno."—Yes! this is all that can with truth be told. The Cav. Clementini should have kept to this, and have spared the feelings of his celestial patrons. We thus arrive at the only known historical fact as previously narrated by the Anonimo Riminese, that Paolo was found by Gianciotto along with Francesca, and that he slew them both.

By introducing, contrary to the authority of Dante, of Boccaccio, and also of Benvenuto, a long interval of time between the fatal kiss and the final catastrophe, the panderers to a perverted sense commit another "brutto fallo," in causing the jealous and energetic Gianciotto—"vir corpore deformis, sed animo audax et ferox"—as Benvenuto describes him, to connive for a time at his wife's infidelity, and patiently to endure the most degrading of injuries. Even Jacopo della Lana and his followers fall into this error, as we may see in the Vendeliniana and the Nidobeatina, the former of which has " correptane più volte dal suo marito non sène casticava, in fine trovolli in sul peccato," etc. ; the latter, "corretta più volte dal marito non se ne castigava, tanto andarono cōtinuando che furono colti sul fatto dal marito," etc. That Francesca and Paolo were slain together in the act of adultery was, we know, the report at the time ; that the supposed long continuance of this adultery should have found its way into the early commentaries cannot surprise us, for the reading, " e il modo ancor m' offende," gave a seeming confirmation to it, and the credulity of the age supplied the rest. But the evidence of Boccaccio, who made diligent inquiry into the subject, shows that the report was false; and so far was Gianciotto from patiently enduring such a dishonour from his own brother, that no sooner was he informed by a domestic of something suspicious having been observed between Paolo and Francesca, than he became "*fieramente turbato*," and, without waiting for a second notice, hurried at once to the spot, to see for himself, and to revenge the injury.

The domestic familiarity which the servant had observed, and of which he promised to give his master ocular demonstration, does not necessarily imply more than Dante has related; and it is obvious, from Boccaccio's account, that this "dimestichezza," this amusing themselves together alone, "senza alcuno sospetto,"

"Soli eravamo e senz' alcun sospetto,"

cannot be construed into criminality, Boccaccio's words, "quasi senza alcuno sospetto insieme cominciarono ad usare,"* meaning no more than is expressed by Dante, Boccaccio having most positively stated that he had never heard any other account of their intimacy. Francesca and Paolo

---

* Boccaccio here employs the verb *usare* in the same sense as Giovanni Villani in his Chronicles, Lib. IV., c. 5.—"E di triegua in triegua si cominciarono à dimesticare i cittadini insieme, e usare l' uno con l' altro nella città di Fiesole e in quella di Firenze."

were much attached to each other, and, thinking no harm, did not disguise their affection. Dante, in placing them among those shades whom love had caused to be deprived of life, depicts them as being easily carried away by the emotion,

"E paion sì al vento esser leggieri;"

but we are not thence to infer that they became so familiar in their affectionate intercourse, as to forget that they were not legally man and wife.

That Francesca's love was a soul abiding and a spiritual affection, we have the testimony of Dante, for in that world of truth beyond the grave described by him, where there is no self-delusion, no corporeal reality, Francesca clings to Paolo still, and can rejoice in this, that his spirit will never more be separated from her own.

From what Boccaccio relates, it is evident, that the unsuspecting though incautious familiarity of Francesca with Paolo was made known to Gianciotto very soon after it had been observed, very soon after its commencement; and this was the opinion held by Benvenuto da Imola.

What followed the intimation given by the servant to his master is well known to all students of Dante.

The sequel is soon told. Gianciotto returns to his palace suddenly and secretly, the servant is on the watch, Paolo is seen to enter the apartment of Francesca, Gianciotto apprized of it hastens to the spot, the door is fastened, he calls, and tries to force it open, Francesca and Paolo are alarmed, and while the former comes forward to open the door, the latter seeks to reach the room below by a secret descent; Gianciotto, maddened with rage, rushes forward, sword in hand, the dress of Paolo has been caught by a nail and he remains suspended, Gianciotto sees him, there is no time for explanation, entreaties are disregarded, Gianciotto strikes at his brother, Francesca throws herself before him, and the blade is buried in her own bosom. The wretched husband " siccome colui che più che se medesimo amava la donna," frantic at the frightful result, withdraws the weapon reeking with the blood of his beloved wife, which, only through her body, had reached that of Paolo, and the tragedy is completed by his death.

Have not domestic deeds of vengeance, the dreadful acts of jealousy, enraged through false suspicions, often stained the Italian soil with innocent blood, and may not this have been one of them ?

Might not the infuriated jealousy of a doting husband, excited by the instigations of a villanous domestic, through a fatal self-delusion, have transformed a suspected criminality into the evidence of confirmed guilt ?—and the dreadful murder having been committed, were there not motives for covering the crime with the report most favourable to the murderer ?

It has been shown that this report, as recorded in commentaries and chronicles, will not stand the test of criticism, will not bear analysis, but is found contradictory, at variance with itself, at variance with the well-attested character of Gianciotto, and at variance with the Dante-drawn portrait of Francesca his wife.

But it will here be asked, ' If Francesca and Paolo were innocent of the crime imputed to them, or if Dante believed they were, or desired that they should be thought so, why did he put these innocent persons in Hell ? '

To this it may be replied, that Dante did believe them to be innocent of this crime, or at least would have his readers think so—for if these lovers had been killed " ambos, unum super aliam, amplexatos," as Serravalle has it, then was this act, as regards Paolo, not murder, but homicide committed under the greatest of provocations, and Francesca, speaking with the prophetic certainty of a disembodied soul, could not truly say, in reference to that murderer who slew his brother because he was more righteous than himself—

> " Caina attende chi in vita ci spense."

Francesca is here the object of Dante's profound commiseration :—

> " Francesca ! i tuoi martiri
> A lagrimar mi fanno tristo e pio ;"

and Virgil does not correct him for it, nor say, as on another occasion—

> " Qui vive la pietà quando è ben morta."

a sure indication that her's was an exceptional case, and that she deserved the world's compassion, not its condemnation.

We cannot expect to fathom entirely the deep mind of Dante. He may have had motives for thus introducing Francesca and Paolo, which we are not able to reach. Their deaths, when he wrote, were in the memories of many; the story that had been circulated about them was commonly received; he might, therefore, have placed them among those shades

"Ch' amor di nostra vita dipartille,"

not only because this was the class under which they thus came, but also because it was the fittest place to obtain for them a hearing, and to vindicate the character of Francesca in the eyes of a world which had unjustly judged and ungenerously condemned her.

Thus we find Achilles placed here also, although he was slain through seeking in honourable matrimony the hand of his beloved Polyxena.

Francesca and Paolo had prematurely perished through love; their deaths had been sudden; there was no time to recommend their souls to God, nor to receive absolution; they had been precipitated by a blow into the place of those

"Che la ragion sommettono al talento,"

and thus had not died in that state of grace which was regarded as the necessary condition of reception into heaven.

The following morning, says Boccaccio, their bodies were interred together, in the same sepulchre, with many tears.

Benvenuto da Imola tells us it was in the church of S. Agostino, and there, according to Andrea Corsucci, in the sixteenth century, when the church was restored, were found together, buried beneath a pier, the bodies of two young persons, one that of a female of rank, in a dress of red velvet and silk, the other of a cavalier, with his sword at his side: they were conjectured to be the remains of Francesca da Rimini and of Paolo Malatesta, and were re-interred, but in what part of the church is not known.

In 1847 I sought to ascertain if anything could now be learnt of them, and on entering the church of S. Agostino, addressed my inquiries on the subject to the Arciprete, who informed me, with much gravity, that, when the church was restored, the bodies of two saints were found beneath the altar, and were not disturbed; and this was all he knew of the matter, and all that he had ever heard.

Were these the bodies of Love's martyred victims? If so, the reality of their sacred rest might, perhaps, in some way compensate their manes for the poetical retribution assigned them.

Many were the palaces in Rimini possessed by the Malatesti, but the one in which this tragedy took place was probably that which once stood in the Piazza, in front of the fortress, on the site now occupied by the new theatre. I was indebted for this, and other information on the subject, to the Signor Domenico Paolucci, Secretary to the Comune of Rimini, a learned and most courteous gentleman, whose personal kindness I have much pleasure in remembering, and his name in recording.

Francesca, it would appear, bore to Gianciotto two children: Francesco, who died an infant (but is supposed by some uncertain), and Concordia, who survived her father.

Deeply did the Polentani deem the honour of their house to have been injured by the cruelty of Gianciotto, the inference that was drawn from it, and the report that was spread. This also it was which so offended the shade of the murdered Francesca— " quia dicor mortua fuisse per adulterium, et causa mei mortuum fuisse Paulum."

Clementini relates that Stefano Colonna, then Papal Rector in Romagna, was also much distressed at it, and had great difficulty in reconciling the two families. But before the close of the year 1290, we find that Malatesta, in company with Guido da Polenta and their friends, seized the city of Forlì, so that according to the chronology of Clementini, who places the death of Francesca in 1289, their enmity was of short duration, though from the cause of offence given we might suppose that it would have taken years to allay.

The Count Uberto, the son of Paolo, resolved to revenge his father's death. He grew up a spirited and chivalrous youth, and early excited the suspicions of his uncle, so that he determined to rid himself of so dangerous a relative. The Count, aware of this, retired to his own estates, and became a distinguished captain of the Ghibellins. He appears to have inherited the mild character of Paolo, added to the military energy of his ancient house, but, like his amiable parent, too incautious and confiding, eventually, through his generous assurance, he fell a victim to the daggers of assassins, the bastard sons of him who slew his father. He was murdered at a supper at the Cava di Ciola, not far from Roncofreddo, to which he had been invited for the purpose, and his body being put into a sack, was taken by night to Rimini, and thrown into the Piazza de' Brandi, where it was found the next morning by some of his friends, and being brought to Ghiaggiuolo, was there honourably buried.

The gentle, generous, and unsuspecting Francesca found in Paolo il Bello a soul congenial to her own, and she loved him from first to last with the natural constancy of a woman's heart; it may be also with the imaginary purity of an angel's intellect, just, as we are bound to believe, Beatrice loved Dante, and Dante loved her;—Boccaccio, be it remembered, is witness for them both. There is, however, a certain difference between them. Beatrice assures us with unerring verity that nothing in nature and in art ever delighted Dante so much as the members of her beautiful body :—

> " Mai non t' appresentò natura ed arte
>   Piacer, quanto le belle membra in ch' io
>   Rinchiusa fui, e che son terra sparte : "

and she rebukes him for it ; but Francesca is more generous, and alluding to the beauty of her former person, pays Paolo a pretty compliment for falling in love with it :—

> " Amor che al cor gentil ratto s'apprende,
>   Prese costui della bella persona
>   Che mi fu tolta, e il mondo ancor m'offende."

With the sweet allurements of love is mingled the bitter remembrance of her sudden death and the injury done to her reputation ; and, as in the speech of Beatrice, where the perishable nature of corporeal beauty is so vividly set forth, the poet, desirous to impress this truth permanently on the reader's mind, has reserved it for the concluding words, so here also in the complaint of Francesca, the climax of her mental suffering is reached in the last sentence, and the greatest weight is thus given to the important assertion touching the cause of her untimely end, that the malicious credulity of the world did her a grievous wrong in receiving as true the reported account of it.

THE MALATESTI.

" E 'l Mastin vecchio, e 'l nuovo da Verrucchio,
Che fecer di Montagna il mal governo."

INFERNO, Canto xxvii., v. 46-47.

THE family of the Malatesti would appear to have been of German origin. Christoforo Zaroto, in his genealogies of illustrious German families, states that its founder's name was Hunifridus, a member of the Habsburg family, and who was called Malatesta from the extreme severity of his disposition; his words are " Ex Geltruda et Otberto Comite Habsburgi, à quo ducunt originem Comites Habsburgenses, nati sunt Hunifridus, cognominatus Malatesta propter eius severissimam naturam." It is possible that the German name, Hunifridus or Hunfridus, may have been a diminutive of Hundfrigidus, meaning thereby a cold-hearted dog; certain it is that " *il Mastin vecchio*," no less than, " *il nuovo*," retained this character of their German ancestor, and Dante may have had reason to give them the appropriate epithet, " *Mastin*," (Mastino), no less from their tyrannical character, than from their original cognomen.

In 998, when the Emperor Otho III. came into Italy to put down the false Pope, John XVII., and to restore peace and order to the land, a process, it would seem, rendered periodically necessary, Hunfridus came with him, and so greatly assisted his master in carrying out his intentions, that he was rewarded with the important post of Imperial Vicar in Rimini, and received from the grateful Monarch various castles and estates. This appointment was confirmed by the Emperor Henry II. in 1009. But the more recent, and perhaps more authentic history of the Malatesti, dates from the close of the twelfth century, where Malatesta della Penna de' Billi, in Montefeltro, there exercised, on his paternal estate, a local jurisdiction. In 1216 he became a citizen of Rimini, and subsequently going to reside at Verrucchio, another castle that belonged to him, about ten miles from the City, took a distinctive title from that place. It is by some affirmed, that this castle had been given to him by the Riminesi, for having, on his return from the Holy Land, delivered their city from an attack made upon it by the Schiavonians; but be this as it may, he was elected Podestà of Rimini in 1247, and died in 1248, leaving two sons, Guido, who died early, and Malatesta, "*il Mastin vecchio,*" who succeeded to his father's titles and estates.

This Malatesta was a very remarkable man, and

early conceived the idea of raising himself to the chief authority in Rimini, a scheme he finally effected by a change of political principles, and a steady pursuit of his purpose without any principle at all save that of personal ambition. He was born in 1212, or, perhaps, in 1210; there is a slight doubt in the date of the year. In the thirteenth century Rimini was the usual residence of the Imperial Vicar in Romagna, and a strong Ghibellin influence prevailed in that city. Malatesta had for some time been wavering in his politics; the defeat of the Emperor Frederick II. before Parma in 1248, where many noble citizens of Rimini were slain, appears to have decided him to take the side of the Church, the Guelf or Papal party affording, as he thought, the best prospect of realizing his ambitious views. In 1250 he came to reside in Rimini. The head of the Ghibellin party in Rimini was Messer Parcitade, whose daughter had been married to Messer Righetto de' Pandolfini da Vicenza, Imperial Vicar in Romagna. The Guelf party was strong, but had no leader; to remedy this, Malatesta was elected to be the head of it, and, becoming its Rector, for his better protection, says the Riminese Chronicler, built that large palace which is close by the Vescovado, and looks towards Verrucchio.

In the meantime Messer Righetto had died, leaving an only daughter, Concordia, a wealthy heiress.

The Guelf party grew and prospered, which

gave much uneasiness to their opponents, the Ghibellins, and Messer Parcitade being alarmed, hoped to gain Malatesta over to his interests by giving him his wealthy granddaughter, Concordia, in marriage. He did so, but the effect turned out quite different to what he had anticipated; it increased the influence and power of Malatesta to the injury of his own; for that astute person, who covered his dark designs with such apparent generosity, that he was called Messer Malatesta il Magnifico, took advantage of this circumstance to work out more effectually the ruin of the man, who had hoped to overreach him by becoming his near relative.

The affairs of the Guelfs and Ghibellins were subject to vicissitudes, often very sudden in their operation, the conquerors of to-day might be the conquered of to-morrow; and the city which had submitted to the authority of the one might suddenly transfer itself to that of the other; for the opposing factions, whom the same walls surrounded, lived for the most part in mutual mistrust, and were often at open war together.

It was many years before the deep scheming Malatesta arrived at the consummation of his wishes.

From the time of his coming to live in Rimini, forty-five years elapsed before he accomplished his purpose. During that period he and his family were occasionally exiles, and were involved in many and dangerous struggles.

Not until the close of 1295 were the Ghibellins finally driven from Rimini, and the authority of the Guelfs established instead, with Messer Malatesta il Magnifico at their head.

The circumstance that brought this great event about was singularly insignificant. Rimini, the ancient seat of the imperial Vicariato, and long the head quarters of Ghibellinism in Romagna, was for ever lost to the empire through the braying of an ass. This was the exciting cause of a tumult which ended in the effectual destruction of the imperial authority.

It happened on Saturday, the 10th of December, 1295, that an ass, followed by the male, loudly braying, entered the market-place at Rimini, amid the shouts and jeers and laughter of the crowd.

The factions were at the time in mutual fear, and kept a strict watch over each other. The uproar alarmed them; each party believed that the other had made a sudden attack upon itself, and both flew to arms. Messer Lodovico dal Caurinate hastened armed into the Piazza, shouting " Viva Messer Malatesta! viva la parte Guelfa!" and was shot dead by a balestriere of Messer Parcitade. This led to a battle that lasted three days, the result of which, but for the duplicity and deep cunning of Malatesta, would have been very different to what it was.

On the third day of the fight, when the parties were still pretty equally matched, and had hard work of it, a secret message was brought to Malatesta that the Conte Guido, a strenuous Ghibellin, had left Urbino with three hundred horse and five hundred foot, to succour Messer Parcitade, who had sent to him for assistance.

This accession to the party of the Ghibellins would most effectually have turned the fortune of the day against the Guelfs. Malatesta was in a critical position, but his art did not fail him. On receiving the intelligence, he caused several of the more peaceable citizens, who were of neither party, to come before him, to whom he expressed himself with such deep concern for the misfortune which had befallen the city, so sincerely regretted the injury done to it through the enmity of the opposite faction, which he said had made an unprovoked attack upon his own, that these good men, persuaded of the sincerity of his sentiments, hastened to report them to Messer Parcitade who, being himself in a strait, the Conte Guido and his forces not having yet arrived, was glad to reciprocate their benevolent tendency, and professed that he had had no intention whatever of attacking Messer Malatesta; the quarrel he said was not his, he never desired it, and did not begin it, and no one could deplore the consequences of it more than he himself did. The good men, who desired the welfare of their city above all party considerations, delighted at the prospect of peace, caused the mutual sentiments of the leaders to be spread among their followers, whereupon the combat ceased, the fight was staid, and the city spared from further injury. Then hope took the place of fear, joy of sorrow, love of hatred: the two chiefs met, they embraced, they kissed; Herod and Pilate were made friends; and chairs having been brought for their accommodation, they were carried on the shoulders of the people into the Palace of the Comune amid universal vivas and shouts of admiration.

In the Palace of the Comune the chiefs renewed their protestations of perpetual good-will; they then got on horseback, a procession was formed, and they rode through the streets of the city demonstrating their attachment.

Party animosities being thus laid aside, and peace happily proclaimed, Messer Parcitade sent to the Conte Guido to say, he thanked him for the intended succour, but no longer required it; on hearing which the Conte Guido laughed very heartily.

In the meantime all strangers who had come to fight for either party were commanded to depart, and trumpeters went round to carry out the order.

As a proof of his sincerity, Malatesta not only sent his people away home to Verrucchio, but rode at the head of them himself on their way back.

The more attached of his friends and followers remained in his palace.

Three miles distant from Rimini, at a place called Mavone, Malatesta ordered his people to halt. At midnight he returned with them secretly,

D

and entered the City by the Porta del Gattolo, the key of which he had taken away in his pocket.

At the preconcerted signal his personal friends sallied forth from their hiding-place, and great was the consternation of the unprotected and unsuspecting Ghibellins: in vain their attempt to stem the torrent of this midnight treachery; "Muoia! Muoia Parcitade!" was the death shout of their murderous enemies; and great slaughter of them is said to have taken place. Among those who fell was a son of Parcitade, named Ugolino; among the prisoners taken was his kinsman, Montagna, a person of considerable importance, who being delivered over into the safe keeping of Malatestino, was subsequently, at the instigation of his father, cruelly put to death with many others.

The chief Ghibellin families fled for their lives, and Messer Parcitade escaped by a garden-gate. On reaching San Marino he was met and welcomed by the Conte Guido with the bitter sarcasm, "Ben venga Messer Perdecittade:" he ended his days in Venice.

Thus the Malatesti became Lords of Rimini on the festival of St. Lucy, the 13th day of December, 1295. Five years after this, they received the title of Vicars of Holy Church.

Malatesta died in 1312; his eldest son, Giovanni (Gianciotto), had died in 1304; Paolo was slain by his brother many years previously; and Malatestino, his third son, by Concordia, to whom on his death the government of Rimini devolved, survived him only five years.

Malatestino

"Quel traditor che vede pur con l' uno,"

is described by Benvenuto da Imola as "astutissimus tyrannus," and his father as "miles audax."

Of "*Mastino*," Benvenuto says, "quasi velit dicere magni magistri Tyrannidis. Mastinus enim fortis est et violentus et rapax qui non de facili dimittit prædam quam assumit." A character which agrees well with these Malatesti, father and son, whose family name had lost nothing of its appropriate sense in the days of Dante.

Marco Battaglia, however, says of Malatesta,— "Hic fuit probus, sapiens, et in omnibus virtuosus, et semper cum fortuna in omnibus suadebat merito :" a statement by no means calculated to increase our faith in Marco Battaglia. Nor is the Anonimo Riminese, a much better guide touching the merits of Malatestino, called "*dell' occhio, perchè era manco d'un occhio*, having lost an eye through a fall when a child ; he describes him as a valiant, wise, and worthy man, who could see more with his one eye than most other people could with their two. He had but a single failing, and that seemed constitutional —he could never behold a Ghibellin without a sensation of nausea.

This was the "*tiranno fello*" who caused the "*duo miglior di Fano*." (Inf. xxviii. 76.) Guido del Casero and Angiolello da Cagnano, whom he had invited to a personal interview at Cattolica, to be murdered on the way, and their bodies thrown into the sea.

Pandolfo, son of Malatesta by his wife Margherita, daughter of Messer Pandolfo di Pesce, succeeded Malatestino as Lord of Rimini. He was of the same stamp as his brother, though the Anonimo Riminese calls him " *molto virtuoso.*"

The atrocious assassination, under his orders, of his nephew, the Conte Uberto di Ghiaggiuolo, at the entertainment to which he had been invited for that purpose, is sufficient to show that the family name as much became him as it did his progenitor.

Paolo was of a different disposition. He is represented by Dante as of a sensitive and amiable temperament; and the evidence from history would show that he had as little sympathy for the ambitious projects of his father and brothers as he had for the violent and atrocious means by which they were carried out. Handsome, affectionate, and esteemed in his day, he was by nature, no less than by education, a more fit companion for the gentle, loving, and confiding Francesca, than was that personification of rapine, outrage and murder, her revengeful husband.

THE END.